PJ MASKS

PJ MASKS SAVE LUNAR NEW YEAR!

Simon Spotlight

New York London Toronto Sydney New D[...]

SIMON SPOTLIGHT
An imprint of Simon & Schuster Children's Publishing Division
1230 Avenue of the Americas, New York, New York 10020
This Simon Spotlight paperback edition December 2021
Adapted by May Nakamura from the series PJ Masks

An Yu is having a peaceful day on Mystery Mountain when an intruder bumps into her. It's Munki-gu, the mischievous monkey!

An Yu tries to stop him, but Munki-gu chants, "Too late, too late, I stole from you. Can't catch me, I'm Munki-gu!"

He holds up a mysterious green bottle, then disappears off the mountain.

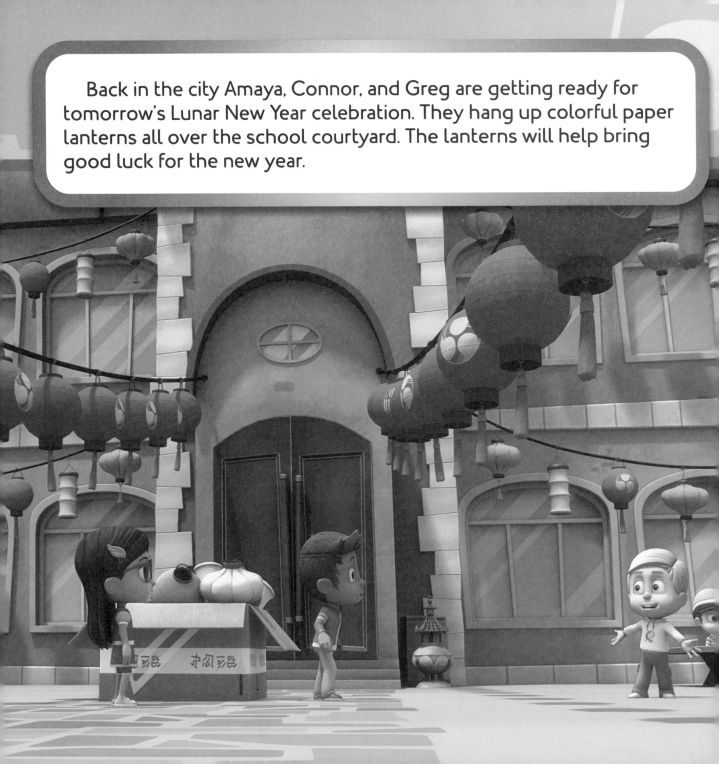

Back in the city Amaya, Connor, and Greg are getting ready for tomorrow's Lunar New Year celebration. They hang up colorful paper lanterns all over the school courtyard. The lanterns will help bring good luck for the new year.

Greg decorates his lizard float for the parade. Then Amaya notices paw prints on the side of the float.

"We can't let villains ruin Lunar New Year," she says.

This is a job for the PJ Masks!

Amaya becomes Owlette!

Connor becomes Catboy!

Greg becomes Gekko!

THEY ARE THE PJ MASKS!

The PJ Masks rush to HQ. They are surprised to see An Yu waiting for them.

"I came to warn you. Trouble is brewing," she says.

PJ Robot chirps and points to the PJ Picture Player, which shows Munki-gu zooming through the streets on Gekko's float!

"That naughty monkey took a magical potion. I'm not sure what it does . . . but knowing him, it cannot be good," An Yu says. She wants to help, but her staff gets its energy from Mystery Mountain. She feels powerless in the city.

"Don't feel bad. Team PJ will take care of it!" Owlette says.

The PJ Masks and An Yu find Munki-gu in the street.
"Give back the float," Catboy says. "And the potion, too."
Instead, Munki-gu unscrews the bottle and pours the potion all
over the float!

The float begins to glow red. Then it rises into the air! The potion in the bottle had been dragon potion!

"Munki-gu wants a dragon for fun, fun, fun!" he says. "Let the monkey dragon tricks begin!"

An Yu points her staff at Munki-gu, but it has no power. Munki-gu giggles and rides away on the dragon.

An Yu decides to return to Mystery Mountain and learn more about the potion while the PJ Masks chase after Munki-gu.

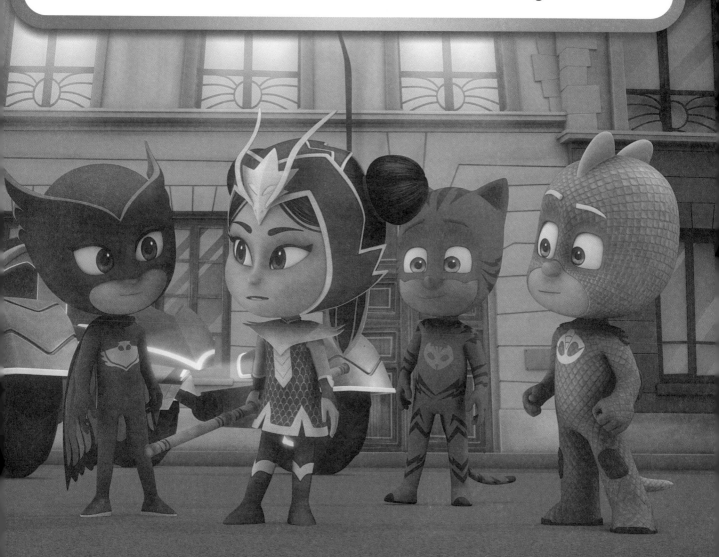

The PJ Masks try to block Munki-gu's path with the Gekko-Mobile. Then the dragon roars and blows puffs of mysterious green smoke, nearly hitting the PJ Masks.

"Wriggling reptiles!" Gekko shouts.

An Yu returns from Mystery Mountain with an ancient book. It says that a dragon like Munki-gu's cannot be defeated for a thousand years unless an ancient dragon riddle is solved:

To fight a dragon with fiery eyes,
prepare yourself for a friendly surprise.

Gekko, Owlette, and Catboy have no idea what the riddle means.

Meanwhile, Munki-gu and the dragon continue to zip around the city. "Munki-gu say, dragon do!" Munki-gu chants. "Faster, faster!"

But the dragon is tired of obeying Munki-gu's orders. It roars at him too. Frightened, Munki-gu runs away into the night.

The dragon finds the PJ Masks and An Yu. It charges toward the Gekko-Mobile and exhales. The Gekko-Mobile is now covered in a cloud of mysterious green smoke!

"That ring of smoke will surround your Gekko-Mobile for a thousand years," An Yu says.

The PJ Masks must think of a way to stop the dragon before the entire city is cursed!

Owlette has an idea. If An Yu stands near the portal that leads to Mystery Mountain, her staff can draw power from the mountain. The PJ Masks can lead the dragon to the portal, and An Yu can defeat the dragon!

"Super Owl Feathers!" Owlette creates a fence of feathers to block the dragon's path and steer him toward the portal.

But the dragon is too powerful. It breaks through the fence, nearly hitting Owlette with green smoke.

"Super Cat Speed!" Catboy tries to lead the dragon, but it is faster than he thinks. The dragon catches up to the three PJ Masks!

"Super Gekko Shield!" Gekko protects them from the dragon's breath, but he cannot hold it off for long.

The PJ Masks and the dragon are still far from the portal. An Yu takes a deep breath. Whether or not she has powers, she must protect her friends in danger!

An Yu runs towards the PJ Masks. Just then her staff begins to glow with energy. She points it at the dragon, sending the green smoke away. "Dragon curse, be gone!" she shouts.

The dragon's fiery eyes stop glowing, and it turns back into a regular float. The cursed smoke surrounding the Gekko-Mobile disappears too.

"The mountain must have sensed my need to help my friends," An Yu says.

The solution to the ancient dragon riddle had been the power of friendship!

"It is Lunar New Year! A special time when friends come together," Owlette says.

But Munki-gu isn't finished with his mischief for the night. There is still some dragon potion left in the bottle. "More monkey fun!" he says with a giggle.

An Yu points her staff at Munki-gu, causing him to drop the bottle and scamper away. She picks up the bottle so it doesn't fall into the wrong hands again.

"Let's take the dragon float back to the school so everyone can have a fun Lunar New Year tomorrow!" Owlette says.

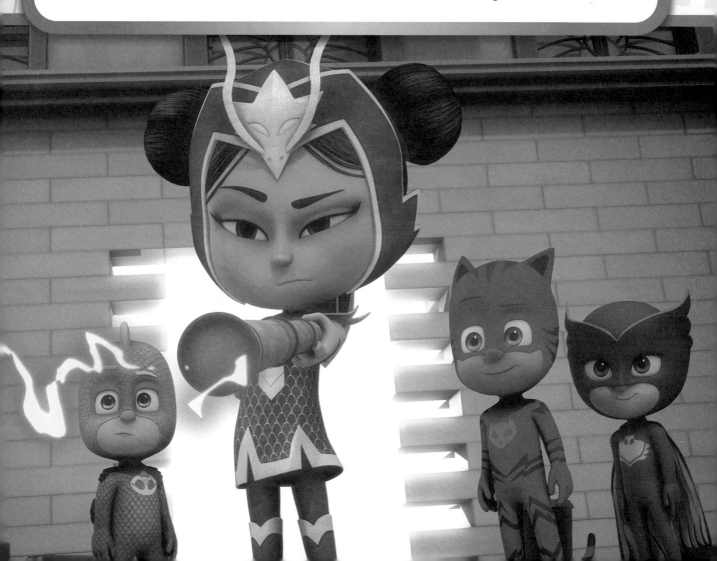

PJ Masks all shout hooray! Because in the night, they saved the day . . . and Lunar New Year!